Sox the Fox

by Bobby Lynn Maslen
pictures by John R. Maslen

Scholastic Inc.
New York • Toronto • London • Auckland • Sydney • Mexico City • New Delhi • Hong Kong • Buenos Aires

Available Bob Books®:

Set 1: Beginning Readers — With consistent new sounds added gradually, your new reader is gently introduced to all the letters of the alphabet. They can soon say, "I read the whole book!®"

Set 2: Advancing Beginners — The use of three-letter words and consistent vowel sounds in slightly longer stories build skill and confidence.

Set 3: Word Families — Consonant blends, endings and a few sight words advance reading skills while the use of word families keep reading manageable.

Set 4: Complex Words — Longer books and complex words engage young readers as proficiency advances.

Set 5: Long Vowels — Silent e and other vowel blends build young readers' vocabulary and aptitude.

Bob Books® Collections:

Collection 1 — Includes Set 1: Beginning Readers and part of Set 2: Advancing Beginners

Collection 2 — Includes part of Set 2: Advancing Beginners and Set 3: Word Families

Collection 3 — Includes Set 4: Complex Words and Set 5: Long Vowels

Ask for Bob Books at your local bookstore, or visit www.bobbooks.com.

ISBN 0-545-02684-1

6 5 4 3 2 1   7 8 9 10 11/0

Printed in China
This edition first printing, September 2007

Sox was a fox.

Sox saw a hen.
Yum! Yum!

Sox hid, but the hen saw Sox.

The hen met a rat.
"Run, Rat!"

The rat met a cat.
"Run, Cat!"

The cat met a dog.
"Run, Dog!"

The dog met a pig
"Run, Pig!"

The rat, cat, dog, and pig ran,

but the hen sat.

"Run, Hen! Run!"

The hen ran.

The fox did not get the hen.

The End

List of 23 words in <u>Sox the Fox</u>

<u>Short Vowels</u>

<u>Aa</u>	<u>Ee</u>	<u>Ii</u>	<u>Oo</u>	<u>Uu</u>	<u>sight</u>
and	end	did	dog	but	a
cat	hen	hid	fox	run	saw
ran	get	pig	not	yum	the
rat	met		Sox		was
sat					